Introduction

In the restless year of 1941, Germany blazed a path across Europe. Joe DiMaggio dazzled crowds on diamond fields, and Emperor Halie Selassie returned to Addis Ababa in triumph. FDR entered his third term as President of the United States, Seaborg and McMillan discovered plutonium, and a wise-cracking, cartoon bunny became the delight of young and old for years to come.

Yet on Christmas Day in the quiet mountain town of Knifley, Kentucky, Virginia Ruth was born to James and Alice Williams. James worked the long, lonely days and nights of a pullman porter for the railroad, while Alice remained to farm and make a cozy home for her aging father and Sweet Ginny.

This is Life in Knifley.

Imani Works!
Human Rights Advocates Since 1996

Life in Knifley: The Hawk

Illustrations: Jason Laudadio

Text: Virginia Cooper with Verdena Lee

Copyright © Imani Works 2012

ISBN: 978-0-9852561-2-8

Life in Knifley

~ The Hawk ~

By Virginia Cooper

Illustrated by Jason Laudadio

One bright day in Knifley, Sweet Ginny woke to the call of the farm's rooster,

"Cock-a-doodle doo!
I need to eat some food.
The hens and I are awake.
How about you?"

Ginny climbed out of bed, washed her smiling face and looked through her window at the chicken coop.

The rooster looked back at her through the window of the latched door and said,

"Cock-a-doodle dee!
A hawk is in the tree.
Did he have breakfast yet,
Or will he eat me?"

In a flurry, the hens began to make some noise to scare the hawk away. It was an awful noise, a terrible noise. They clucked and flapped inside the coop until feathers and dust floated through the window.

Sweet Ginny rushed to the kitchen
where Mamma was wearing her apron.
She was busy making 5 large apple pies for the butcher.

"Mamma, there's a hawk in the tree right by the coop. And the chickens are afraid!" said Sweet Ginny. Then she began to run around in circles in the small hot kitchen where the smell of butter, sugar and eggs filled the air.

She ran around and around. She flapped her arms pretending to make dust and feathers fly.

And then, Sweet Ginny suddenly jumped to a stop.
She stood as tall as she could with her chest stuck out,
her shoulders back and called,

"Cock-a-doodle doo!"

Sitting in the chair that he and Sweet Ginny caned, Grandaddy smiled.

As his smile grew along the rim of his raised coffee cup, he took a good, slow sip.

Mamma chuckled until her shoulder shook.
But she never missed a beat of slicing
the apples for the 5 large pies.
Before Mamma could
say a word,

Sweet Ginny flew through the screened door
and into the yard by the coop.

She ran to the coop clucking and flapping and kicking up dust. She joined the cackling chorus of the hens led by the rooster. The sound of their piercing song climbed from the yard, through the coop and up the tree.

The song climbed so high it reached the hawk's ears.

But he could not stand the terrible sound. So he spread his wings, jumped from the tree and flew away down the mountain.

Sweet Ginny stood still watching the hawk retreat.
She was dusty and out of breath.
And once she was sure the hawk was gone,
she unlatched the tall coop door.

The rooster flew out first and perched on the
wooden fence Grandaddy built years ago.
All the hens ran out of the coop and gathered around Sweet Ginny's knees.

Each hen sang her own special coo of joy. And all began to dance. Together,
they skipped around the chicken run as the rooster crowed and sang,

"Cock-a-doodle die!
The hawk sat up high.
He didn't like our song,
so away he did fly."

"Cock-a-doodle day!
The hawk is on his way.
He flew down the mountain this time.
But he'll come another day.

Grandaddy asked Mamma, "Where did Ginny go?
Her grits are going to get cold."
Looking outside beyond Grandaddy's sight
at her little girl dancing with the hens,

Mamma said.

"Oh, she went to let the chickens out for me
while I bake the butcher's pies.
She'll be in again soon."

About Ginny

Sweet Ginny was born December 25, 1941

in the mountains of Kentucky.

About the Author

Virginia (Williams) Cooper grew up in the Cumberland Gap region of Kentucky in the town of Knifley. She moved to Akron, Ohio where she worked as a teller while tending her family and raising her three daughters. Today, she serves as a Mother in a national church organization where she shares the wisdom she learned so long ago and where her husband Albert Cooper is a presiding Bishop. The "Life In Knifley" series is written with the assistance of her youngest daughter Verdena Lee.

About the Illustrator

Jason Laudadio is an illustrator that enjoys working in a wide variety of styles and always has a warm place in his heart for Children's books. If you would like to see more of his work please visit www.laudadio.ca.